CRUSTACEAN VACATION

Written by
BRIAN BENOIT

Illustrated by
MARTY KELLEY

PUBLISHED BY

Islandport Press
P.O. Box 10
267 U.S. Route One, Suite B
Yarmouth, Maine 04096

books@islandportpress.com
www.islandportpress.com

ISBN: 978-1-934031-95-7
Library of Congress Control Number: 2011935508
Printed in China.
January 2012
Plant & Location: Everbest Printing Co. Ltd. Nansha, China
Job #105723 / Batch 1

ISLANDPORT PRESS   YARMOUTH • MAINE

For Emery and Liam,
once and future crablets
—*Brian Benoit*

For all my friends,
even the crabby ones
—*Marty Kelley*

CRUSTACEAN VACATION

Written by
BRIAN BENOIT

Illustrated by
MARTY KELLEY

From out of the sea, from out of the spray,
The crab family's going on holiday!

With one eye to starboard
and one eye to port,
The crab family looks
for a seaside resort.

While Dad lounges poolside

and Mom hits the spa,

The two little crablets play "What's in my Claw?"

The crabs go in search of an afternoon treat:
Peanut butter and jellyfish - bon appetit!

Without any warning or hint of a blow,
The crabs are dismayed to find lunch is To Go!

Sticky with ketchup and pink lemonade,
The crabs go explore a boardwalk arcade.

He's daring! He's dashing!
With strength seldom seen,

The daddy crab wrestles
a taffy machine.

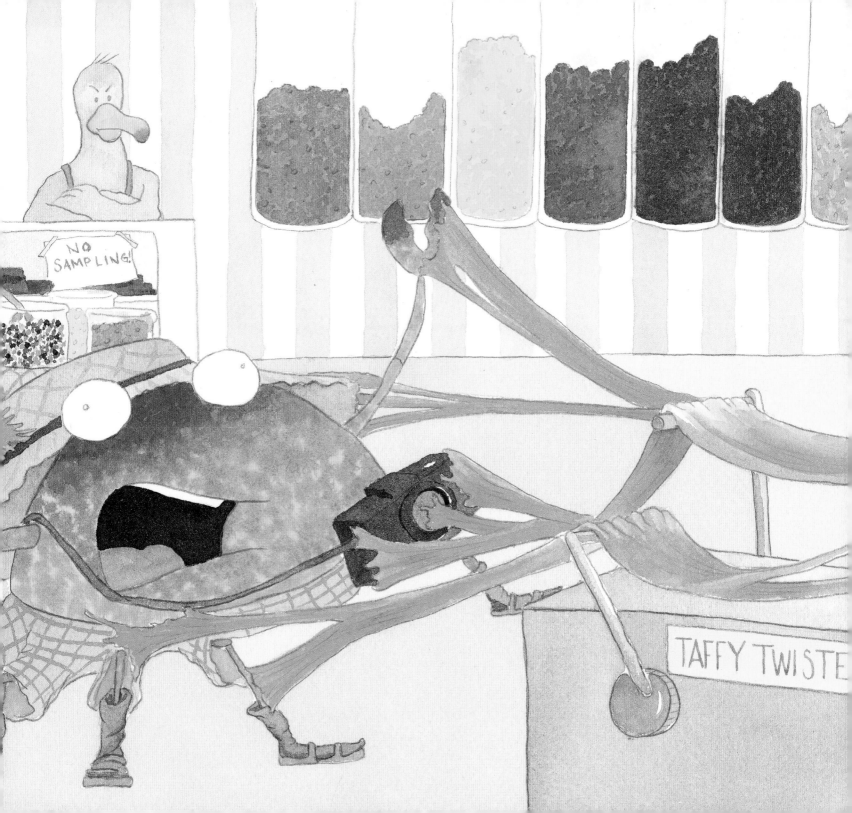

A game with a crane that both scuttles and grabs

Was plainly designed for the mind of a crab.

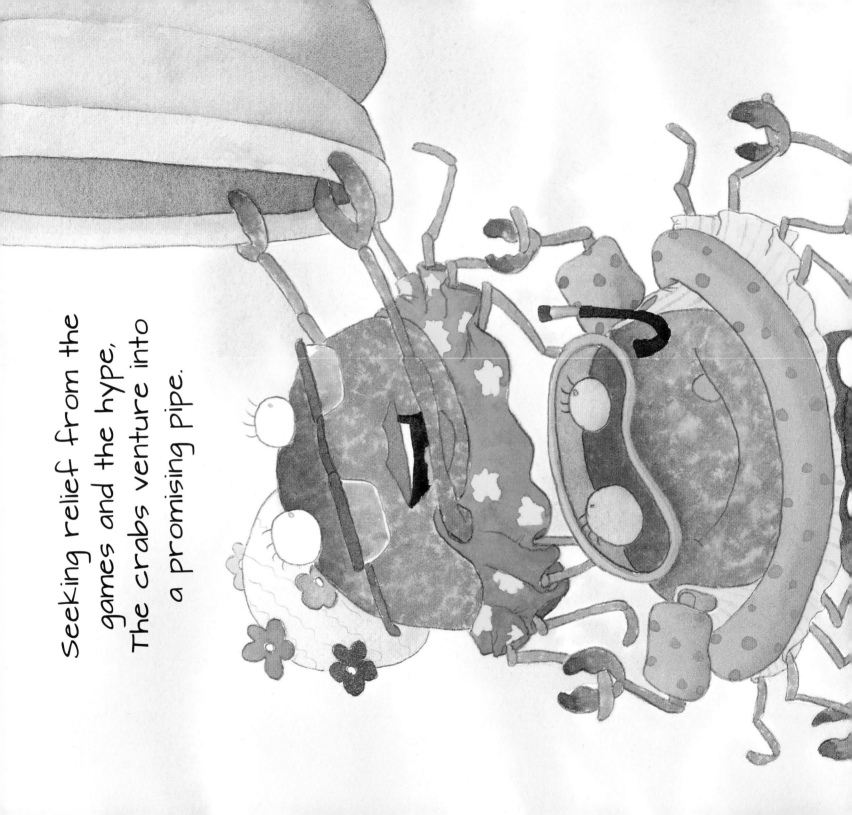

Seeking relief from the
games and the hype,
The crabs venture into
a promising pipe.

Awe-struck, incredulous,
thanking their grandma,
The crabs find themselves
in crustacean nirvana.

Never in crabulous, undersea dreams

Have crabs encountered such heavenly streams!

Small crabs go big and big crabs go huge,

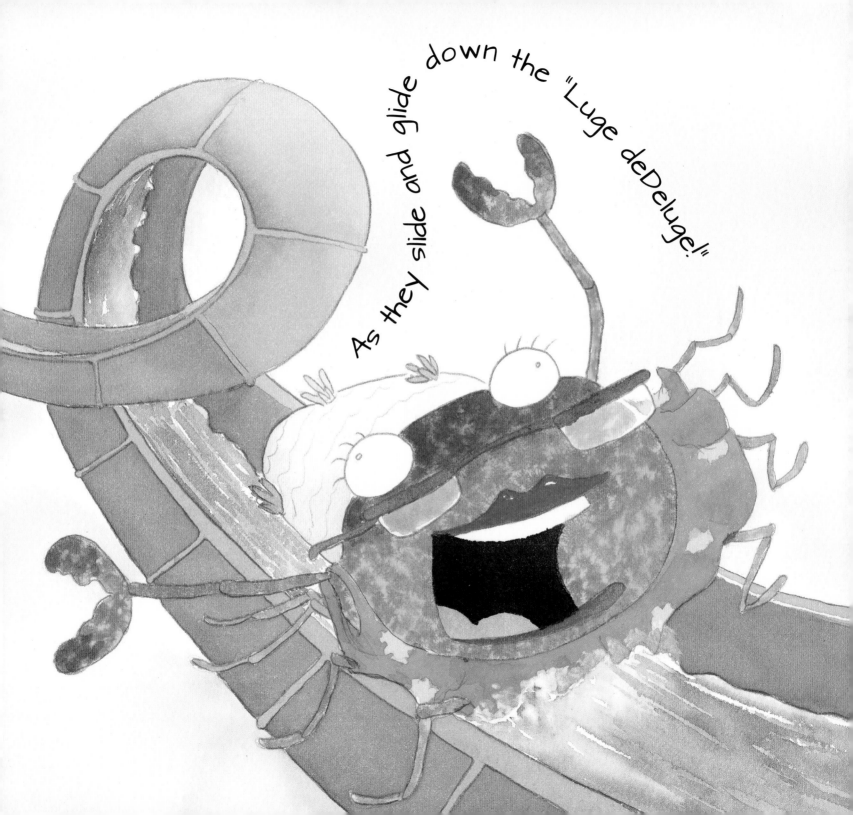

Grownups exhausted,
the kids shouting "More!",

The crab family makes its way back to the shore.

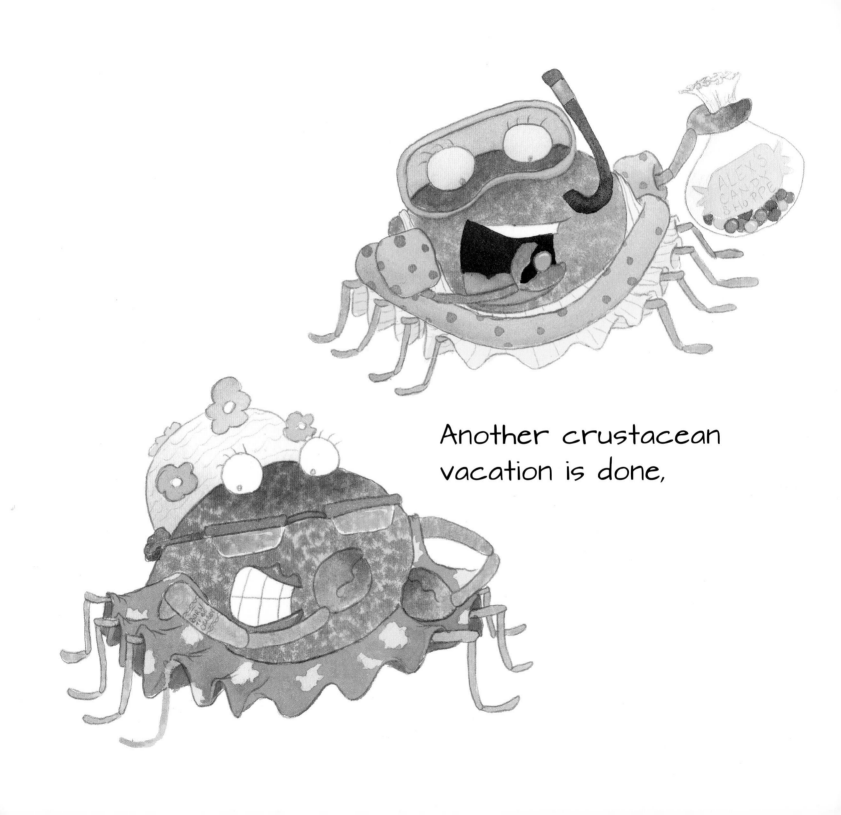

Another crustacean
vacation is done,

Filled with marvelous
memories of
fun in the sun.

About the Author

Originally from Somersworth, New Hampshire, author Brian Benoit now listens for the roar of the surf deep in the woods of Cavendish, Vermont. His sea creatures were originally conjured up to entertain his brother during family trips on the Maine coast, but have since proven popular with his own children. He finds inspiration in the poetry of Ogden Nash, Shel Silverstein, T.S. Eliot, Edward Lear and Lewis Carroll. When he's not playing with language, he indexes historical government documents for NewsBank/Readex. He shares his life with his wife, Jennifer; daughter, Emery; and son, Liam. *Crustacean Vacation* is his first children's book.

About the Illustrator

Marty Kelley is the author and illustrator of several children's books, including *Fall Is Not Easy*, *The Rules*, *Winter Woes*, *Summer Stinks*, *Spring Goes Squish*, *The Messiest Desk*, and *Twelve Terrible Things*. His career as an artist started when he began drawing historically accurate pictures of spaceships dropping bombs on dinosaurs. He has, in the past, been a second grade teacher, a baker, a cartoonist, a newspaper art director, a drummer in a heavy metal band, a balloon delivery guy, and an animator. Now he visits lots and lots of schools to show students how he creates his books. He is also a juried member of the New Hampshire State Council for the Arts Visiting Artist Roster, and represented New Hampshire at the 2011 National Book Festival. For more, visit www.martykelley.com.